MICHAEL DAHL PRESENTS
SCARY STORIES

WEREWOLF HOTEL

BY STEVE BREZENOFF

ILLUSTRATED BY NEIL EVANS

STONE ARCH BOOKS
a capstone imprint

Michael Dahl Presents is published by Stone Arch Books,
an imprint of Capstone.
1710 Roe Crest Drive
North Mankato, Minnesota 56003
www.capstonepub.com

Library of Congress Cataloging-in-Publication Data is available on the Library
of Congress website.

ISBN: 978-1-4965-9717-5 (library binding)
ISBN: 978-1-4965-9894-3 (paperback)
ISBN: 978-1-4965-9736-6 (eBook PDF)

Summary: The Full Moon Hotel and Resort in western Canada looks all but
abandoned when Hunter, his twin sister, Maeve, and their parents arrive. The
outdoor pool is in disrepair and the cabins are overgrown with strange plants.
What a dump! And to make matters worse, Hunter and Maeve's aunt and uncle,
as well as their two kids, fail to show up for the family vacation. What is going
on, and why did they have to come all the way out to the sticks anyway?
Before long, the spooked-out siblings find out why—and it's a very hairy
situation indeed!

Designer: Hilary Wacholz

Printed in the United States of America.
P0117

MICHAEL
DAHL
PRESENTS

Michael Dahl has written about werewolves, magicians, and superheroes. He loves funny books, scary books, and mysterious books. Every Michael Dahl Presents book is chosen by Michael himself and written by an author he loves. The books are about favorite subjects like monster aliens, haunted houses, farting pigs, or magical powers that go haywire. Read on!

SHARE THE FEAR!

You are not alone. And I don't mean that a creature
lurks in the dark shadows of your bedroom. Or a slimy
menace lives under your bed. (Although that might
be true.) I mean, you are not alone in being afraid.
Everyone is afraid of something. Every. Single. Person.
Reading about other people's fears in these weird tales,
you might learn how to overcome your own.
Or you might learn how to escape from zombie teachers
attacking the school. Both are good things to know.
Just be sure to leave the lights on while reading!

Michael Dahl

TABLE OF CONTENTS

Chapter 1

THE RESORT IN THE WOODS

The Nord family's SUV rolled over the bumpy driveway toward the Full Moon Hotel and Resort.

"Haven't these people heard of pavement?" said twelve-year-old Hunter Nord from the back seat.

"This place is a dump," said his twin sister, Maeve.

The rutted, muddy driveway curved around a dirty, unused pool. Next to it was a small dirt parking lot.

Dad parked close to the main building. Only one other car sat in the lot. It was an old pickup truck with huge tires.

"Not a popular place," Dad said, grabbing two suitcases from the back of the vehicle.

"Looks like Uncle Edgar's family isn't here yet either," Maeve pointed out.

"They probably took one look at the place and fled," Hunter joked.

"If you three are going to bad-mouth this place all weekend," Mom said, "just drop me off and go home. You're forgetting—"

Mom stopped for a moment—out of breath. She put a hand on the hood of the car.

"You're forgetting," she went on, still leaning on the car, "I grew up near here . . ."

"You okay, Mom?" Hunter asked. He hurried over and took her arm to steady her.

"Oh my," she said. "I feel pretty woozy."

"Let's get you inside," Dad said. "Kids, help Mom into the lobby."

Hunter held her elbow, and Maeve took her other arm.

"You probably got out of the car too fast," Maeve said.

The main hotel was an old four-story brick building. Its massive copper roof was green with age. Against the building sat a garden of tall plants with spiraling purple flowers.

Mom lost her footing and crumbled to her knees. Hunter and Maeve hoisted her with their shoulders. Together, they got her inside and laid her down on a bench in the lobby.

"Maeve, find some wet paper towels in the bathroom," Dad said. "Hunter, you stay with Mom. I'll see if I can find someone who works here."

Hunter sat on the edge of the bench and held Mom's hand. "You okay?" he asked.

She blinked. "Probably just dehydrated," she said.

It had been a long morning. First the flight up to Dawson, and then the long drive.

"Your mother?" said a rough voice.

Hunter spun around. In the open doorway stood a man with a face as rough as tree bark. He wore heavy denim pants and a flannel shirt and hat. In one hand, he carried a long landscaping tool with a shiny, pointed head.

"Yes," Hunter said. "She'll be okay in a few minutes."

"You must be the Nord family," the man said gruffly. "I've got your cabin all ready for you."

Chapter 2

WAIT TILL MORNING

Cabin Four sat just inside the woods on the far side of the parking area. The log building was short and wide.

A narrow garden grew against the front of the cabin and around the porch. It boasted the same spiraling purple flowers planted around the main house.

Calvin Deere—the gruff man Hunter met in the lobby—unlocked the front door and swung it open.

They entered to find a small living room with a couch and an old-fashioned TV. At the back was a kitchen. The doors to the bedrooms stood open.

Calvin handed the keys to Hunter's dad.

"And you haven't heard anything from the other family we made a reservation with?" Mom asked him. She pressed the wet paper towel against her pale forehead.

"No," Calvin said shortly. He stepped off the porch and, without looking back, added, "Checkout is ten a.m."

"He doesn't seem to want us here," Maeve pointed out.

"Well, that makes three of us, then," Hunter quipped.

"So he's a little odd," Mom said as she sat on the couch. "He probably doesn't have to deal with people very often."

"He runs a hotel!" Hunter pointed out.

"But not a very popular one," Maeve said.

"Let's get unpacked," Dad said. "I'm sure your cousins will be here any minute."

* * *

Unpacking didn't take long, and after just a few minutes of rest Mom was feeling better too.

Dad sent Hunter and Maeve with a few dollars to the main building for snacks.

"Well, howdy," said the woman behind the desk. "You must be the Nords."

"The Nords, yup," Hunter said. "I'm Hunter, and this is my sister, Maeve."

"I'm Krystal Deere," the woman said. She had long, white hair with gray streaks.

Around her neck hung a simple leather band. Three long, sharp teeth dangled from it like charms.

"Is Calvin your husband?" Maeve asked.

The woman laughed. "He's my brother," she said. "Getting settled okay? Need anything?"

"We were hoping for some food, actually," Hunter said.

The woman smiled. Hunter thought she seemed friendlier than her brother.

"We sell candy bars and cans of soda here at the desk," Krystal said.

"What about healthier food?" Maeve asked.

"Well," Krystal said, peeking under the counter. "I've got some beef jerky."

"We're vegetarian," Maeve said.

"Don't get many vegetarians around here," Krystal said. "You'll have to drive into Garou for food, then. The service station has a couple aisles of groceries and a freezer."

"Come on," Hunter said, grabbing Maeve's hand. "Let's get Dad to drive us into town."

"I wouldn't bother today," Krystal called after them as they walked away. "The sun's nearly down."

"So?" Hunter asked, turning back toward the desk.

"The service station will be closed," Krystal said. She smiled, but to Hunter it seemed forced.

"What if someone needs gas?" Maeve asked.

"We have a saying around here," Krystal said. For a moment, her face seemed to darken. "'It better wait till morning.'"

"But why?" Hunter asked. "Is the area haunted or something?"

"No," Krystal said. Her forced smile came back. "But it's not safe, and it's not something you kids need to hear."

"Tell us," Hunter said.

Krystal shook her head. Then she reached under the desk and pulled out two chocolate bars and two sodas. "On the house," she said. "Get back to your parents now. It is starting to get dark."

Krystal just stood there grinning—her hands clasped tightly, her knuckles turning white—until they left.

Chapter 3

WALKING IN THE DARK

The sun was low now. With the tall woods all around and no streetlamps, it seemed much darker. Only the full moon, hidden behind streaky clouds, lit up the property.

A chill settled over the area. Hunter shivered. Maeve pressed against his shoulder as they made their way across the resort's dirt parking lot.

The ice-cold soda in his hand sent a shiver through Hunter's whole body. He felt Maeve beside him shiver as well.

Cabin Four seemed miles away, a single dim porch light at the edge of an endless darkness.

"We should hurry," Maeve said.

"Why?" Hunter said. "Remember what Mom always told us at bedtime when we were little?"

Maeve nodded. "Everything in the dark," she recalled, "was there in the light too."

"Right," Hunter said as they walked on.

An owl cried from not far away. Something scurried behind them.

"What was that?" Maeve whispered.

"It's nothing," Hunter said. "Just a raccoon or something the owl scared."

The rustle came again. It sounded like someone—or something—moving through the woods around them.

"Mr. Deere?" Maeve called out softly. "Is that you?"

Hunter shushed her. "Quiet," he said. He strained to listen. No more rustling.

"It's gone," Maeve whispered. "Whatever it was."

Hunter listened to their footsteps on the dirt. Then his breath caught. He grabbed Maeve to stop her.

"Wait," Hunter hissed. Their footsteps stopped, but a scraping sound along the parking lot behind them continued.

"Run!" Hunter shouted.

The twins dropped their sodas and bolted the rest of the way. They leapt onto the porch and slammed through the door.

Chapter 4

MONSTER AT THE WINDOW

Mom and Dad both looked up as the twins stood there, out of breath. Hunter pressed his back against the door as if a monster was about to smash it down.

"What happened?" Dad asked. He hurried to them, his face twisted with panic.

"It's nothing," Hunter admitted quickly. "We thought we heard something outside."

"We got spooked," Maeve said.

"Especially with that weird stuff Krystal was telling us," Hunter said.

"The owner?" Dad said. He pulled Maeve into a hug. "What did she tell you?"

"Nothing, really," Maeve said.

"Just that Garou shuts down after dark," Hunter said.

"Did she say why?" Mom said.

Hunter shook his head. "But it seemed like something scary," he said.

"Wow," Mom said, putting her fists on her hips. "After all these years, people are still spreading the old stories."

"Honey," Dad said, "let's wait until your brother's family arrives, okay?"

"I'm just glad we finally came up here," Mom said, nodding. She sat at the small kitchen table and picked up her coffee mug. "I never should have left."

"Left?" Hunter asked.

"I grew up here," Mom said. "Well, not here at the resort. In Garou. My dad worked in the lumber mill."

She laughed lightly. "Everyone's dad did, really. When the mill closed, we left. It's hard to believe I'm back."

* * *

An hour later, Hunter lay in the darkness. From the other bed, he heard Maeve's gentle breathing. He also listened to the owls crying and crickets chirping. Then all went silent.

Hunter strained to listen, but the whole forest seemed to have shut down. Nothing stirred. Nothing sang. Nothing even moved.

Something must have scared the animals, Hunter thought.

"Maeve," Hunter whispered into the darkness. She didn't answer.

Hunter watched the window over his sister's bed. It glowed pale blue under the big, bright full moon.

Then a burst of wind shook the branches outside the cabin. They scratched the building like clawed fingers.

A shadow flickered past the window.

"Maeve!" Hunter said, louder than last time. She didn't even stir.

Hunter grabbed his phone from the nightstand. It was after midnight.

As Hunter walked carefully across the room, the wind howled again. The scratching branches outside the cabin made him jump.

He crept to the window and slowly pulled aside the window shade. In the pale moonlight, Hunter could see the gnarly trunks of young pines. He could see the lower branches swinging in the wind.

He pressed his face against the glass. Outside, nothing stirred. Hunter waited several minutes, and soon an owl called. The crickets chirped again.

Hunter felt his shoulders relax, and his breathing returned to normal.

Maeve sat up. She put her face next to his. "What are you doing?" she asked.

"I heard something," Hunter said.

Maeve pressed her face against the window next to Hunter's. "Seems pretty quiet," she said.

"It was probably nothing," Hunter said. "Just everything suddenly got quiet out—"

Bam! Something slammed against the window.

Hunter and Maeve fell back and screamed. As the window's shade rolled up with a snap, a wolf's snarling face glowed in the moonlight. It barked and slobbered, steaming up the window with its hot breath and splattering spit.

Bam! Bam! Bam! The beast slammed its face against the window, snarling and growling.

"It's going to smash the window!" Maeve shouted.

The twins huddled together in the middle of the floor and closed their eyes in terror.

"Dad!" Hunter yelled. Maeve shrieked.

The window finally gave in with a smash. Shattered glass sprayed into the room.

Hunter and Maeve screamed.

Chapter 5

WOLVES ALL AROUND

The door slammed open, and Hunter looked up. Dad stood in the open doorway and switched on the light.

A tree branch poked into the room through the broken window. Wind rushed in, and the window shade fluttered wildly. Pine needles littered the floor.

"What happened?" Dad asked. He rushed to the window and looked out.

"Dad, no!" Hunter said.

But his dad looked relieved.

"It's nothing to worry about," Dad said. "Just a tree branch that someone should have trimmed back ages ago."

He picked up a shard of glass from Maeve's bed. "It's lucky no one got hurt," Dad said. "I've got half a mind to wake up Mr. Deere right now."

"No, Dad," Hunter said. "It wasn't the tree branch that broke the window. It was a wolf."

Dad furrowed his brow. He looked at Maeve.

She nodded. "It's true," she said.

"A wolf?" Dad repeated as Mom came into the room, pulling her bathrobe tightly closed.

Her face fell and went pale. "What about a wolf?" she said.

"Nothing, nothing," Dad insisted. "The kids had quite a scare. A tree branch just slapped the window and shattered it."

"It wasn't a tree, Mom," Hunter said. "It was a wolf. I saw it."

"I saw it too," Maeve said.

"They're scared," Dad said. "There's the branch that did it." He pointed at the broken window.

"There *are* wolves around here, you know," Mom pointed out, raising an eyebrow. Something went unspoken between Mom and Dad, but Hunter couldn't imagine what.

"Yes, well, now isn't the time to get into it," Dad said. "It's the middle of the night."

Dad turned to Hunter and Maeve. He smiled, but his eyes looked sad—the way they got on their birthdays and first days of school.

"Dad," Maeve said, "what's up?"

"You're not telling us something," Hunter said.

"Let's just get you two to bed," he said. "You'll take our room. Mom and I will sleep on the foldout couch. Anything else can wait until tomorrow."

Maeve took his hand. "Dad, please," she said.

"Tomorrow," Dad said. "We'll talk about it tomorrow."

"But—" Hunter protested.

"Enough." Dad cut him off. "Go to bed."

Chapter 6

THE MILL

The twins woke up late the next day. Dad had already been to Garou for groceries, and after a very late breakfast, it was already the middle of the afternoon.

Hunter and Maeve stood on the cabin's porch as Calvin plodded across the dirt lot.

"Hi, Mr. Deere," Maeve called. "Here to fix the window?"

Calvin carried a big section of plywood

and an old-fashioned red toolbox. He walked hunched over, more like a beast than a man.

Without replying, the caretaker walked right past the twins and into the cabin.

A moment later, Dad came outside.

"How about a walk in the woods, guys?" Dad said. "There's a lake not far, I think."

"Sure," Hunter said. He loved hikes.

"Isn't Mom coming?" Maeve asked.

"Mom's not feeling well today," Dad said. "Probably just needs to get some sleep."

Dad handed them each a water bottle. "There's a path right around back," he said.

Hunter followed slowly. He kept his eyes on the ground, looking for any evidence of last night. All he saw, though, were wet leaves, snapped branches, and shards of broken glass under the window.

The branch that Dad blamed for the smashed window had already been cut.

Under the window, Hunter only saw big boot tracks. If there had been wolf tracks, Calvin must have messed them up when he was cutting the branch.

Hunter looked up at the window. Calvin stood there looking down at him. His gray eyes seemed icy and mean. His pale lips bent into a gnarly, toothy snarl.

"Taking a hike?" Calvin asked. He didn't wait for an answer, but went on. "Better be back before the moon rises."

"Hustle up, Hunter!" Dad called. He and Maeve were already well ahead on the path.

"I'm coming," Hunter said. He jogged to catch up.

* * *

"Where's that lake already?" Hunter asked. The sun was getting low.

"Yeah," Maeve said. "I'm getting tired."

The trail they started on had been marked and lined with wood chips to keep it clear. Now, though, the trail seemed more like a worn rut weaving through the trees.

Not far off—less than one hundred feet or so—Hunter saw a wide, red building surrounded by trees. Its windows were covered with dirt where they weren't broken.

"What's that?" Hunter asked, nodding toward the building.

"That's the old lumber mill," Dad said. "It's why I brought you out here today."

"Why didn't you say so?" Maeve asked.

"I didn't want Calvin to hear," Dad admitted. They stepped out of the woods and stood in front of the old mill.

"Many years ago," Dad said, "when Mom was a little girl, they closed this place down."

"Why?" Hunter asked. "There are still plenty of trees to cut down."

"Because of the accidents," Dad said.

"Did people get hurt?" Maeve asked.

"Yes," Dad said, rubbing his chin. "Very badly—but then accidents are bound to happen at lumber mills. Trouble is, the mill didn't close because of a poor safety record. It closed because the people of Garou believed the accidents weren't really accidents at all."

"What *did* they think they were?" Hunter asked.

"Werewolves," Dad said in a grim voice. "They said a pack of werewolves lived in the woods nearby. They said the werewolves attacked any lumber mill worker who stuck around after the moon was up."

"And that's why everything closes at dark?" Hunter asked.

Dad nodded. He paced slowly away, as if lost in thought.

"Werewolves," Hunter whispered to Maeve. "Based on last night, I think the stories are true."

"Are you kidding?" Maeve said. "Mom and Dad wouldn't bring us to a place with real werewolves prowling around."

"I don't know," Hunter said. "They've been acting really weird. And didn't you see that necklace Krystal was wearing?"

"With the teeth?" Maeve said.

Hunter nodded. "Probably her own baby werewolf teeth or something," he said. "And Calvin was super-creepy this morning. He warned me to be back before the moon rose."

"He wasn't exactly friendly yesterday

either," Maeve said. "You think he's planning to hunt us?"

Hunter didn't answer. He just thought about Calvin's beastly walk and toothy grin.

"Hey, look," Maeve said. She nodded toward the big, dirt parking lot. "A car."

Hunter turned. It was an old station wagon.

Hunter and Maeve jogged over to it. A dark puddle shone in the sunlight. Half the puddle was under the car.

"Looks like it sprang a leak," Hunter said. "Someone probably had to spend the night here at the mill."

Maeve knelt beside the puddle and dragged her finger through it. She lifted her finger and shook her head.

"It's not oil," she said, as a bright-red liquid ran down her finger. "It's blood."

Chapter 7

COUSINS

"What's going on?" Dad asked as he placed his hands on the twins' shoulders.

"I think someone is hurt," Maeve said. She held up her finger to show him the blood.

"This is Uncle Edgar's car," Dad said, staring at the puddle under the car.

"We'll get help!" Hunter said. He and Maeve sprinted into the woods.

"No!" Dad said. "There's no need to—"

But the twins ignored Dad's protests. Something terrible must have happened to their cousins.

"It was werewolves," Hunter said breathlessly as they ran along the hiking trail.

"It's daytime," Maeve said.

"Then it was last night," Hunter said. "I'm telling you: that wolf at the window was Calvin. *He* did something to Uncle Edgar's family."

The twins weaved through the woods. After what seemed like an hour, Hunter burst out of the trail and across the dirt parking lot. He skidded to a stop.

Parked right next to their family's SUV was the same station wagon they had found at the mill.

"I don't believe it. That's Uncle Edgar's car," Maeve whispered. "But how?"

"We beat you here," said Uncle Edgar as he came around from the other side of the car. He wore a heavy-looking backpack. "We did have a car, after all."

Aunt Rieka opened the passenger door and climbed out. "We stopped at the mill to show the kids," she said. "We saw your dad vanish into the woods as we got back to our car."

The back door opened, and cousins Caleb and Jessamine climbed out. Both hugged Hunter and then Maeve.

"It's great to see you," Uncle Edgar said, leaning against the car. "Where's your mom?"

"But there was blood," Hunter murmured.

"What's that?" Aunt Rieka asked.

Hunter didn't get the chance to explain.

"Ed!" came Mom's voice from behind the twins.

Mom burst out of the cabin and started down the porch steps. But she only made it a few feet before she stumbled and fell.

Hunter hurried to her side, but Uncle Edgar was faster.

"Easy there," Uncle Edgar said quietly.

"I've been trying to reach you since we got here," Mom said. "Where were you?"

Uncle Edgar shrugged one shoulder. "Rieka and I wanted to show the kids our old stomping grounds," he said.

"The mill?" Mom said. "Ed, we were going to talk with my kids first."

"We had no choice," Uncle Edgar said. "Surely you've noticed the gardens around this resort. We didn't want to get too close unless we had to."

Mom slapped her forehead. "Of course," she said. "That's why I've been so ill."

"You're a little out of practice, sis," Uncle Edgar said, helping Mom to her feet.

"Anyway," Uncle Edgar said, "the hunting near the mill is terrific. Caleb brought down his first deer."

"The blood we saw," Hunter whispered to Maeve. "It must have been from the deer."

"Gross!" Maeve replied.

Uncle Edgar led Mom to his car and helped her sit in Aunt Rieka's seat. Mom seemed to be getting stronger already.

"Where's that husband of yours?" Uncle Edgar asked.

"Dad should be back any second," Maeve said. "I heard him behind us on the trail."

"Yeah, he couldn't keep up," Hunter said.

"No," Jessamine said with a twinkle in her eye. "I wouldn't think so."

Jessamine was the same age as the twins, while Caleb was three years younger. Both had their mother's narrow blue eyes and their father's dark mop of thick hair.

"Hunter!" came Dad's voice from the trail. "Maeve!" He appeared out of the woods a few moments later.

"When did my two kids get so fast?" Dad said, gasping for breath.

"They're growing up, Kevin," said Uncle Edgar, offering his hand. "How've you been?"

The dads shook hands.

"We saw your car," Dad said, "down at the mill. The kids were worried and ran back." He glanced at Caleb and Jessamine briefly. "I tried to tell them you were fine."

Uncle Edgar smiled at Dad for an awkward moment. Then he put an arm around Hunter and a hand on Maeve's shoulder.

"How about you two show my kids around a little?" Uncle Edgar said to Hunter and Maeve. "Give us grown-ups a chance to catch up."

Hunter looked at his dad for permission. Dad nodded.

"Sure," Hunter said. "Come on. We'll show you the hiking trail. Not much else to see."

"Unless you like disgusting old swimming pools," Maeve added.

Caleb and Jessamine laughed. The four kids headed for the trail.

"And hey!" Uncle Edgar called after them. "Don't pick any flowers, Jessamine. Understand?"

"Yes, Dad," she called back to him. Then, as they stepped into the woods, she added in a whisper to the twins, "He is always on my back about something."

Chapter 8

FULL MOON

They walked along the trail in silence. Though Hunter and Maeve were supposed to be showing their cousins around, Caleb and Jessamine walked in front. They seemed to know where they were going well enough.

"Do you think we should we tell them about the werewolves?" Hunter asked his sister. "It'll be dark soon."

"Nah," Maeve said. "They'll just think we're crazy."

Every so often, Caleb stopped and sniffed loudly.

"What are you doing?" Hunter asked him.

Jessamine gave her little brother a playful punch in the shoulder. "He's got allergies," she said.

They walked on. Soon Hunter noticed the trail was becoming narrow and worn. "We're heading back to the lumber mill," he whispered to Maeve.

"They're leading us right to it," Maeve replied.

Jessamine and Caleb let the twins catch up. "So," Jessamine said, "I heard you two had a scare last night."

"Yeah," Maeve said. "The wind slammed a tree branch through our bedroom window. Scared us half to death."

"Hey, wait a second," Hunter said, facing

Jessamine. "How did you hear about that? You just got here. Our parents haven't even had a chance to catch up."

"My mom talked to your mom on the phone this morning," Jessamine said. But Hunter noticed her cheeks go red as she quickly turned away.

"I'm starving," Jessamine said.

"Me too," Caleb said. "I could eat like ten deer all by myself."

"Eeew," Maeve said. "We don't eat meat."

"We know, we know," Jessamine said. She led the way onward toward the mill. Caleb hurried along at her side.

"Hey," Hunter called after them, "you're going the wrong way. The hotel is back that way."

"Yeah," Maeve said. "The only thing in that direction is the old lumber mill."

Neither of the cousins replied as Hunter watched them weave quickly and gracefully through the trees. Then, as if they had faded into the growth, they were gone.

"Where'd they go?" Maeve asked.

"Let's go find them," Hunter said.

The twins stepped out of the woods. The sun had now set, and the only light came from the full moon.

When they reached the mill's parking lot, they were alone. Jessamine and Caleb were nowhere to be seen.

"Great," Maeve said. "They just got here, and we already got them lost at the creepy old mill."

"Caleb? Jessa?" Hunter called out. "Stop messing around."

A shadowy figure stepped out of the mill's dark doorway.

"Caleb?" Hunter said. "Is that you?"

The figure raised its head, showing off a long snout. Then it howled at the moon.

"Run!" Hunter said.

The creature lunged from the doorway. Hunter dashed to the woods and hid behind a tree. Then he looked around for Maeve.

She must have run in the other direction, he thought.

Hunter pressed his back against the tree trunk and held his breath. Should he risk leaving his hiding spot to find Maeve?

A twig snapped.

"Maeve?" he whispered. "Is that you?"

The undergrowth rustled.

"Who's there?" Hunter said.

Suddenly, a figure leapt out of the darkness with a great roar.

Chapter 9

THE PACK

Jessamine stood there and laughed. "I'm sorry," she said. "I couldn't resist." She put out her hand to help him up.

Hunter shoved it aside.

"Come on," Jessamine said. "We have some food inside."

She led Hunter toward the mill.

"We're not supposed to go in there," Hunter said. "And where's Maeve?"

"She's already inside the mill," Jessamine said. "Let's go in. I'm starving. Aren't you?"

He was. Hunter's stomach tightened as he caught the salty, rich smell of meat on a fire.

Inside, the mill was dark. The only light was a small fire in the farthest corner. He saw Maeve there, sitting with her back to him, silhouetted by the fire's flickering light.

"It's hot in here," Hunter said. He sat down beside his sister.

"The food's really good," she said.

Hunter looked down at his sister's hand. She held a metal skewer of chunks of meat. "We're not supposed to eat meat," he said.

"It's fine, cousin," Caleb said. He now sat on the other side of the fire.

"When did you get here?" Hunter asked.

"I was here the whole time," Caleb said.

Hunter took the skewer. It was warm—not hot—and the meat was still pink. He took a bite. The meat was salty and rich. Deer.

Hunter licked his lips as the juices slid down his throat.

"Caleb," said a voice from behind Hunter, "save some for the rest of us."

Hunter twisted around. Behind him in the big, open doorway stood Mom, Dad, Uncle Edgar, and Aunt Rieka.

"I'm sorry, Mom," Hunter said, suddenly ashamed for having eaten meat.

"I ate some too, Mom," Maeve said. "We're really sorry."

"It's fine," Mom said. She and Dad took each other's hand and walked toward them. "Dad and I talked it over. It's time."

Dad put a hand on Hunter's shoulder. "It's going to be okay," he said with a sad smile.

Then two big dogs trotted toward them.

No, Hunter realized. *Not dogs. Wolves.*

Hunter dropped the skewer. He suddenly felt hot—too hot. He tore off his flannel shirt and tried to rip off his T-shirt. But his hands were . . . wrong somehow.

Hunter couldn't grab the fabric. He snarled in frustration and fell to the floor, writhing.

"Dad," Hunter cried, "what's happening?!"

But no answer was needed. Hunter knew what he was changing into.

His hands became gnarled and hairy. His fingernails bent and thickened into long, wicked-looking claws.

He lowered his head as his nose and mouth pulled from his face into a long snout.

And soon the cavernous mill filled with his chilling and glorious howl.

Chapter 10

THE HUNTERS

Hunter padded across the mill's hard, cold floor. Smells filled his head. Familiar smells. New smells. Complex smells with a wild rainbow of colors.

Hunter closed his eyes. Even without them he could "see" the world around him.

Dad pressed a hand against his cheek. "I can't be what you've become," Dad said. "So I'll have to say goodbye." His words sounded slow and muddy, but Hunter understood.

Hunter barked and sniffed as Maeve padded up beside him. They both jumped at Dad, pressing their muzzles into his neck.

"I'll miss you both," Dad said. "But I knew this day would come. And forcing you to fight who you are would be painful and cruel. You'll be happier in the wilderness."

Hunter knew he was right, but he followed Dad to the door, loyal and faithful.

"Stay here," Dad said. "I'll try to visit."

As Dad stepped out of the mill, Hunter smelled something familiar. It was tangy, with a mix of onions, soap, and soil.

Hunter snarled. Then, as if struck by something, Dad fell backward into the mill with a great thud.

Calvin Deere, looking fearsome and huge, stepped through the doorway. He held a long spear. Its pointed head shone in the moonlight. Krystal stood behind him, gripping a silver-bladed knife.

"I knew it," Calvin said. "The instant the woman fell ill in the parking lot, I knew."

"Wolfsbane," Krystal said. "A werewolf hunter's best friend. We keep it growing around every building. It weakened her."

Uncle Edgar, Aunt Rieka, and Mom—all still human—approached the caretaker.

"Your family has tormented Garou long enough," Calvin said, pointing his spear.

"Nonsense," Mom said. "Who's to say we didn't just hunt animals in these woods?"

"I say," Calvin snarled. "You slaughtered the workers at this mill for decades."

A sinister smile spread across Uncle Edgar's face. "Perhaps those were just machinery accidents," he said. "That was the official explanation."

"Ha!" Calvin spat. He jabbed his spear toward Uncle Edgar. "You expect me to believe a family of werewolves never tasted the blood of this town's people?"

"It no longer matters what you believe," Aunt Rieka said.

Calvin swung his spear at the adults. Maeve snarled and Hunter barked.

"Get them back," Calvin said, jabbing at the twin werewolves with his spear. Then two more werewolves padded up. Jessamine beside Hunter and Caleb next to Maeve.

Calvin and Krystal took a step back, realizing they were outnumbered.

"We'll be back," Calvin said. "We'll bring a posse and end this forever." They turned and ran.

Mom knelt next to her husband.

"What happened?" Dad asked, sitting up.

"Turns out the Deeres are werewolf hunters," Mom told him.

"I should have known," Dad said.

"We must stop them," Mom said with a snarl. Then she, Aunt Rieka, and Uncle Edgar transformed before Dad's eyes.

"No," Dad said. "I won't let my children become murderers. Forget the Deeres and run. Go farther north, deeper into the wild."

Hunter turned to the pack leaders—Uncle Edgar, Aunt Rieka, and his mother. His uncle raised his snout and howled. Then he leapt through the doorway. As the rest of the pack followed, Hunter paused for a moment to press his muzzle against Dad's open palm.

"Go ahead, son," Dad said, scratching the boy's mane. "I'll see you soon."

With a howl, Hunter sprinted into woods—heading north with the pack.

ABOUT THE AUTHOR

Steve Brezenoff is the author of more than fifty middle-grade chapter books, including the Field Trip Mysteries series, the Ravens Pass series of thrillers, and the Return to the Titanic series. He has also written three young adult novels, *Guy in Real Life*; *Brooklyn, Burning*; and *The Absolute Value of -1*. In his spare time, he enjoys video games, cycling, and cooking. Steve lives in Minneapolis with his wife, Beth, and their son and daughter.

ABOUT THE ILLUSTRATOR

Neil Evans is a Welsh illustrator. A lifelong comic art fan, he drifted into children's illustration at art college and has since done plenty of both. He enjoyed a few years as a member of various unheard-of indie rock bands (and as a maker of bizarre small press comics), before settling down to get serious about making a living from illustration. He loves depicting emotion, expression, and body language, and he loves inventing unusual creatures and places. When not hunched over a graphics tablet, he can usually be found hunched over a guitar, or dreaming up book pitches and silly songs with his partner, Susannah. They live together in North Wales.

GLOSSARY

caretaker (KAIR-tay-kur)—a person whose job is to look after a building, property, or other people

cavernous (KA-vuhrn-uhs)—large and open, like a cave

evidence (EV-uh-duhnss)—information, items, and facts that help prove something to be true or false

flannel (FLAN-uhl)—wool or cotton cloth often used to make work shirts

muzzle (MUHZ-uhl)—an animal's nose, mouth, and jaws

reservation (rez-er-VAY-shuhn)—an arrangement to save a room or a seat for someone

sinister (SIN-uh-stur)—looking evil or harmful

torment (TOR-ment)—to cause pain to others

vegetarian (vej-uh-TER-ee-uhn)—a person who does not eat meat

wolfsbane (WULFS-bayn)—a poisonous plant with purple flowers that is often used as a weapon against werewolves in folklore and legends

TALK ABOUT IT

1. In chapter three, Hunter and Maeve get scared when they hear rustling and scraping noises around them as they walk back to the cabin. What do you think was making those noises? Why do you think so?

2. Hunter and Maeve get their ability to turn into werewolves from their mom's side of the family. What is a trait you got from one side of your family, but not the other? Describe how that trait makes you like one of your parents.

3. Hunter and Maeve become werewolves and run off into the woods at the end of the story. What do you think about this plot twist? How does it change the way you feel about the main characters?

WRITE ABOUT IT

1. Imagine that you have the ability to turn into a strange creature or monster. Write a paragraph about what you would become and draw a picture of what you would look like.

2. In this story, the Nords stay at the creepy Full Moon Hotel and Resort deep in the Canadian woods. What is the creepiest place you've ever visited? Write a scary story of your own that is set at your creepy location.

3. At the end of the story, Hunter and Maeve turn into werewolves and run into the forest with their pack. But what happens next? Write a new chapter that continues their story.